# A is For Absoloth.

by John Lagnarok Gieg

For Snootch.

First Stillwater River Publications Edition.

Library of Congress Control Number: 2018940232

ISBN-10: 1-946-30051-9
ISBN-13: 978-1-946-30051-5

1 2 3 4 5 6 7 8 9 10

Written by John Leonard Gieg
Published by Stillwater River Publications, Pawtucket, RI, USA.

Publisher's Cataloging-In-Publication Data
(Prepared by The Donohue Group, Inc.)

Names: Gieg, John, 1960- author, illustrator.
Title: A is for Absoloth : [a primer of forgotten gods, monsters & heroes] / by John Lagnarok Gieg.
Description: First Stillwater River Publications edition. | Pawtucket, RI, USA :
    Stillwater River Publications, [2018] | Subtitle from cover.
Identifiers: ISBN 9781946300515 | ISBN 1946300519
Subjects: LCSH: Gods--Fiction. | Monsters--Fiction. | Heroes--Fiction. | Alphabet books. Classification: LCC
PS3607.I2759 A57 2018 | DDC 813/.6--dc23

$\mathbb{A}$ is for Absoloth.

"Solitary Watcher."

"In his house at R'lyeh, dead Cthulhu waits dreaming." A monstrous entity of immense power, Cthulhu abides in a death-sleep in some unimaginably deep oceanic trench.

Untold eons ago, a thousand sentries were set in place to wait and watch for his foretold return. Of these sentries, only Absoloth remains.

B is for Berry Boy.

"Nostalgic Ghost."

Somewhere just beyond human perceptive range is an empty parking garage in what looks very much like the city of Rotterdam, *but isn't.*
Here Berry Boy paces the vast gray vaults, reciting nonsensical poetry in his characteristic mumble.

Rainy nights he plays a Rudy Vallée record over and over again on a haunted victrola. Listen for it.
Berry Boy is the son of Echo, a woodland nymph of Greek mythology, and Jens Halvorsen, the famous Norwegian librarian and literary historian.

# $\mathbb{C}$ is for Clotilde.

"Scholarly Queen."

Free to pursue her studies, Princess Clotilde was happy to be upstaged by her beautiful older sister, Nelga, the "Huntress Queen" of Thulbaria. Clotilde became Queen later in life, after Nelga was trampled during an elk hunt.

The reign of Queen Clotilde saw a steady rise in the small nations' literacy rate and standard of living. Thulbarians in time became famed for their many contributions to science, literature, diplomacy, and the fine arts.

# D is for Disgorgeon.

"Sludge Demon."

The brilliant inventor and playwright, Valporthera, might have politely declined Queen Dhrudallas' amorous advances (and hope for the best). Instead, he openly ridiculed her in his brutal, dark comedy "The Gamy Duchess".

Dhrudalla responded by sending eleven Disgorgeon, (or mung devils), to plague Valporthera. The vile creatures sprayed him with filth whenever he tried to eat or sleep, forcing him to live alone and wretched in an abandoned lighthouse for years.

# E is for Egwald.

*"Royal Clod."*

It wasn't so much that King Egwald ("The Numb") of Ephesia was clumsy, but that he believed he was a master swordsman. He was the last person who should have been entrusted with the enchanted sword, Cleavescabbard, which was ceremoniously presented to him on his thirteenth birthday, the day Egwald became King.

To call someone "graceful as Egwald" is still a serious insult in Ephesia, as it implies extreme stupidity as well as a complete lack of physical skill.

# $\mathbb{F}$ is for Farnsworth.

*"Most Eloquent Waterfowl."*

Le Duck Du Farnsworth (lower right), not only spoke, but was generally considered the greatest orator of the Age of Enlightenment.
Discovered in a travelling circus by a close advisor to Queen Clotilde of Thulbaria, Farnsworth the Talking Duck was brought to court as a novelty but soon proved indispensable as a diplomat.
Farnsworth loved impressive sounding titles.
Her full Thulbarian title was: *"Il Mugnífic Grandé Vox Proclamaré; Le Duc Pâté Du Farnsworth"*.

G is for Sir Glavnar.

"The Golden Mouse Reborn."

The moment he donned the newly excavated armor of the legendary Gylden Mus, Sir Glavnar became invincible. Ridding the land of ogres and wood bloars took Glavnar mere weeks. Neighboring kingdoms took note and chose the path of peace.

Inside the armor, there was all along, a large red button clearly marked with a skull and crossbones. Sir Glavnars' curiosity finally won out.
The resulting explosion left a deep crater three miles wide that we know today as Lake Glavnar.

# H is for Hydrus.

"Silent Crustacean Bodyguard."

"He just *showed up*." whispered the High Chamberlain to Lord Harald of Limerick. After quickly dispatching the royal guard, Hydrus appointed himself Haralds' sole protector. Indeed, none could harm Lewd King Harald while his strange, mute champion lived.

After ten years or so, Hydrus abruptly turned egg-plant purple with bright white spots, curled up in a tight ball and began to stink.
Believed dead, he was wrapped in chains, stuffed in an iron-bound chest and thrown into the North Sea.

I is for Ignatz.

"Broken Golem."

Hephaestus, Greek god of blacksmiths, sculptors, and metallurgy, labored to create a gigantic automaton of bronze. Before he could complete his metal colossus, it was damaged in an earthquake and strode off into the Aegean Sea.

In the ages since, Ignatz the Wanderer has criss-crossed the globe many times over, never stopping, never tiring.
Ignatz has recently been spotted trudging in wide circles in the Gobi desert.

$\mathbb{J}$ is for Julius Boof.

"Fearless Jester."

The life of a court jester was frought with peril, as everything depended on the mood of their ruler. Julius Boof was, at different times, jester to Lord Vragrrad the Vile, Arch Duke Sebastion the Surly, and Queen Dhrudalla the Inconceivably Spiteful.

Boof took risks for his art. Embarrassing his patron at the absolute worst possible moment was at the core of his comedy. It was Boof who came up with the infamous "Fart During Coronation" gag. In spite of himself, Boof lived to a ripe old age.

# K is for Kadia.

"Melodic Saint."

Kadia is the patron saint of spring thunderstorms, marsh warblers, and the proto-sousaphone.
In life a traveling street musician, a young Kadia coaxed a procession of mesmerized fever-demons from Notre Dame cathedral to drown in the river Seine, ending the second plague of Paris in 1352. Accused of witchcraft and sentenced to burning at the stake, Kadia was saved from the flames by a sudden downpour. Many present claimed she was then carried to safety by a confusion of warblers.

𝕃 is for Lotan.

"Pygmy Leviathan."

Lotan were giant catfish that dredged the Euphrates in centuries past.
Babylonian King Nebuchadnezzar, falling overboard his golden throneship, was swallowed whole in a story like that of Jonahs' only better documented.

The lotan soon ran aground, and the King, barely alive, wriggled free of the great maw and in no time had the event declared a miracle.
Celebrations in Babylon went on for weeks, and old Nebuchadnezzar went on to be an even worse King.

# M is for Malanthus.

"Rampaging Glutton."

The list of ancient cities devoured by the dragon Malanthus is horrifically long.
Perhaps most famous was multicolored *Lobbiopolis* in the kingdom of Snackbarvania (depicted here). Lost also, the once proud metropolis of *Tunarolia,* the many tiered capitol of Klamshaq. *Kafeteria* with its bustling throngs. Steep-walled *Taconium. Wafflesssa, Donutonia,* and gleaming *Dinerium* with its hundred plazas of chrome and linoleum. All lost forever to the monsters' appetite.

# N is for Nohochacyum.

"Creator-Destroyer."

Nohochacyum, the chief god of the Maya, god of creation and protection, is brother of the death god Kisin. His other brothers, Usukun, Uyitzin, Yantho, and Hapikern - are all haters of humanity, Nohochacyum is the sworn enemy of his brother Hapikern, the evil god and great serpent. In the end of days, Nohochacyum will destroy Hapikern by wrapping him around his own body to crush and smother him. In some versions of this story, all life on earth is destroyed in the process.

# O is for Ozymandias.

"Unremembered King of Kings."

Time steps on us all equally. It grinds us to dust and continues without pause.
All grandeur is folly and all are consigned to oblivion. All has been done, all has been said. We stumble along a hallway of mirrors in total darkness.

This is one lesson we might take from Ozymandias. Another might be: that even the mightiest of tyrants fall, and, for all their power and bluster, in time, the harm they have brought to the world will be as nothing.

# P is for Porkbeard.

"Pirate Explorer."

April, 6, 1602 - fleeing Portuguese warships, pirate Captain Perry Porkbeard, (true scourge of the seven seas and lord and master of the infamous Bilge Rat), reluctantly sailed into the Lethe region of the Sargasso Sea.

The battered Bilge Rat eventually ran ashore on Monster Island, leaving days later with only half its crew. Like the Polynesian and Viking seamen before them, the traumatised pirates did their best to forget about the whole experience.

Q is for Questing Beast.

"Monstrous Oddity."

Hunted relentlessly by Sir Palomides over many years, the Questing Beast became the object of early scientific inquiry when it was at last slain and its corpse presented at the court of King Anguish of Ireland.

Danthur DeNoblasse, the court Alchemist who dissected the creature, noted:
"A very large beast, bizarre of form and as strange of body as of conformation and as strange inside as outside. From whence did it originate?"

# $\mathbb{R}$ is for Ragnhilda.

"Last Bullockornis."

In 1102, (or thereabout), three Viking longships led by Bjorn the Easily Distracted, approached an uncharted isle, (almost certainly Monster Island), and encountered a creature that fits the description of a Bullockornis, or, "Demon Duck of Doom".

The morning fog parted and their landing was met by a fourteen foot tall, seemingly indestructible man-eating duck with a bill like a great battle-axe. They named her Ragnhilda, after Bjorn's pugnacious half-sister.

$\mathbb{S}$ is for SMOE.

"Sock Monkey of Enlightenment."

It has been said that there are a thousand and one paths to enlightenment. An influential spiritual leader of the ancient world, the Sock Monkey of Enlightenment, (or Smoe), was said to have mastered seven hundred and three such paths.

# $\mathbb{T}$ is for Teutonia.

"Amazon Diva."

There once was a giantess of a fierce tribe who longed to be a famous opera star but, because of her immense size and strength, was pressured to become a warrior.
Unlike most such stories, a compromise was reached.

Teutonia sang like a host of mad Valkyries in the midst of some of the bloodiest fighting imaginable. Her primal, pottery-shattering battle cry triggered mass hysteria among the enemy, and, in at least one instance, brought about an immediate surrender.

$\mathbb{U}$ is for Unhcegila.

"Serpent Monster."

The ancient Lakota tribes of the Northwest had heard rumors from neighboring tribes that a great shadow had emerged from the icy Atlantic waters of the far Northeast.

Unhcegila was her name, and her form was massive, with a long scaly body whose natural armor was almost impenetrable. Her eyes burned with an insatiable hunger and her claws were like iron.

$\mathbb{V}$ is for the Vordunes.

"Crow Feeders."

The majestic gardens of Xeones were silently over-seen by the Vordunes - enchanted constructs made to resemble angelic sisters.
Their intended role was to help guide lost visitors through the mazelike gardens and off the grounds.

As centuries passed and the land was abandoned, the Vordunes became strange and lost sight of their original mission.
The vast, thorny, overgrown labyrinth is even now watched over by their malevolent, mad eyes.

# W is for Werecat.

"Shadow Stalkers."

Werecats predate werewolves by a thousand years, the earliest known reference from an Egyptian scroll from the time of Moses.

While there is mention of a werecat hunt in ancient Persia, and Viking settlements in Britain endured an outbreak of rabid werecats in the 8th century, encounters are rare, as Werecats are extremely stealthy creatures who go to great lengths to avoid people. Without them, the world would have long ago been overrun with wererats and werevoles.

$\mathbb{X}$ is for Xeones.

"Invincible General."

An indentured tunnel worker, Xeones' legend began with his early victories as a rebel leader during the Third Mandolian War, when his small band of starving tin miners defeated the well armed, Elite Corps of Munificent Patriots.

His strategic brilliance was called upon to serve the Grand Republic time and time again, until his final defection to the Thull Empire, whose Emperor, Sabadaar VII, gifted Xeones with a magnificent, *peaceful* garden estate in return for his retirement.

# Y is for Yoshita.

"Fox-Eared Savior."

Yoshita could not speak to the many spirits of the great cedar forest, but, being born with the ears of a fox, she could plainly hear them talking to each other. When the beetle god made plans for the yam field, her timely warning saved the crops.

When drought came, Yoshita Foxears knew where the water spirits made their home.
She anticipated the worst storms, averted enemy invasions, and saved her village from a hundred different hardships.

# Z is for Zorlac.

"Jackal Headed Deity."

Zorlac appears in legends from unrelated cultures across thousands of years. He always looks exactly the same and is always named Zorlac.

To Egyptians, Zorlac was a devious wizard who granted troubled people one wish. This never ended well for them.

To the Maya, Zorlac was a freedom fighter revolting against the ruling gods. To the Iroquois, a helpful spirit who gave farming tips. In 1700's Belgium, he instructed inventors in strange, advanced sciences.

# The Author & Illustrator.

John Lagnarok Gieg has been drawing since he can
remember. Mostly monsters and dragons and such.
His other book, "A Coloring Book of Many Dragons"
is just what it sounds like.
Mr. Gieg lives just outside of Providence, in the
small but feisty state of Rhode Island.
His real middle name is Leonard.